Dear Reader,

My late husband, Stephen, and I started working on *Keep Dancing Through* in the summer of 2021. We wanted the book to reflect our family's values about spreading kindness and hope, our mottoes and daily affirmations. And what a joy it was to work on. We reviewed passes with the kids, who were delighted to see themselves in illustrated form. We read through it hundreds of times, and still had smiles on our faces when we were done. It was a true passion project, a family effort.

Now that the book is finished, I am so proud of what we made, and how it encapsulates our family, how you can feel the real love and joy running through every page. I hope reading it sends a little joy and love to all of you.

And of course, I hope it inspires you to dance. Because, to put it quite simply, that's what our family is going to do—we're going to keep dancing through.

Allison Holker Boss

To Weslie, Maddox, and Zaia—my greatest loves and inspiration
—AHB

To each and every heart yearning to see
the bright side in a tough situation
—SW

Text and illustrations copyright © 2023 by Allison Holker Boss and Stephen Boss
Illustrations by Shellene Wright

First Edition, January 2024
10 9 8 7 6 5 4 3 2 1
FAC-039745-23271
Printed in China

This book is set in Adelon/Fontspring
Designed by Joann Hill
Illustrations created digitally

Library of Congress Cataloging-in-Publication Data

Names: Holker-Boss, Allison, 1988– author. • Boss, Stephen, 1982– author. • Wright, Shellene, illustrator.
Title: Keep dancing through : a Boss family groove / by Allison Holker Boss & Stephen Boss ; illustrated by Shellene Wright.
Description: First edition. • Los Angeles : Disney Hyperion, 2023. • Audience: Ages 3–7. • Audience: Grades PreK–2. • Summary:
Mom, Dad, Weslie, Maddox, and Zaia celebrate their family and their favorite motto—keep dancing through.
Identifiers: LCCN 2022037982 (print) • LCCN 2022037983 (ebook) • ISBN 9781368092197 (hardcover)
ISBN 9781368095761 (ebk)
Subjects: CYAC: Dance—Fiction. • Family life—Fiction
LCGFT: Picture books. Classification: LCC PZ7.1.H64585 Ke 2023 (print)
LCC PZ7.1.H64585 (ebook) • DDC [E]—dc23
LC record available at https://lccn.loc.gov/2022037982
LC ebook record available at https://lccn.loc.gov/2022037983

ISBN 978-1-368-09219-7
Reinforced binding
Visit www.DisneyBooks.com

KEEP DANCING THROUGH

A BOSS FAMILY GROOVE

by Allison Holker Boss and Stephen "tWitch" Boss

Illustrated by Shellene Wright

DISNEP • HYPERION

Los Angeles   New York

Ring ring ring

Jump up, shake a leg!
The Boss family's getting
ready for the day.

Brush brush brush
Maddox bounces.

Drip drip drop
Zaia grooves.

Tick tick tock

Weslie bobs in the mirror.

Step step step

Everybody's on the move.

Munch munch munch

Breakfast time, let's go.

Nudge crash whoops!

Passed the jug without glancing.

Skeet skat skoop

Dad turns on some tunes.

Spin spin spin

But they're already dancing.

I'm strong, smart, and kind.
I've got beats around me too.
Take some deep breaths in and out,
And I'll keep dancing through.

Honk honk honk

Wave to Dad and Weslie.

Trick trick drip

Say hi to Dale and Sue.

Step step slide

And so do their fly shoes.

Remember:

I'm strong, smart, and kind.
I've got beats around me too.
Take some deep breaths in and out,
And I'll keep dancing through.

Bop bop bop

Maddox plays at recess.

Thud thud thud—

But Ben takes his ball!

Sniff sniff sniff

Maddox lets the tears flow.

Tap tap tap

Chooses kindness, standing tall.

I'm strong, smart, and kind.
I've got beats around me too.

Take some deep breaths in and out,
And I'll keep dancing through.

Kick kick kick

After school, meet at the field.

Woo woo woo

Cheering Weslie's soccer game.

Go go go!

They pass, they shoot, about to score . . .

Scritch scritch scritch

Home in time to color.

Shade shade shade

A sun, a teddy bear.

Scoot scoot scoot

Zaia wanted yellow first!

Sniff sniff sniff

Sometimes it's really hard to share.

I'm strong, smart, and kind.

I've got beats around me too.
Take some deep breaths in and out,

And I'll keep dancing through.

Clink chomp chew

Dinner all together.

Splish splosh clank

Then wash the crumbs away.

Whizz whizz whuzz

The family grins
at one another.

Jump jump jump

The perfect way
to end our day.

I'm strong, smart, and kind.
I've got beats around me too.
Take some deep breaths in and out,